This book
belongs to

....

....

First published 1995 by
Chart Books Limited, Chart Warren,
Seal, Sevenoaks, Kent. TN15 0EJ

ISBN 1-899912-03-7 hardback
ISBN 1-899912-04-5 paperback

British Library Cataloguing in Publication Data
A catalogue record for this book is available from
the British Library

Printed in Italy

TALES FROM HENRY'S GARDEN
WILLIE THE WATERING CAN

WRITTEN BY SIMON HICKES

ILLUSTRATED BY JILL BROOKS

CHART
BOOKS

Willie was a watering can. He lived behind the door in the garden shed. He was made of metal and painted green.

His long nose was called a spout. It ended in a round brass bowl called a rose, which he used to spray the plants and flowers with water.

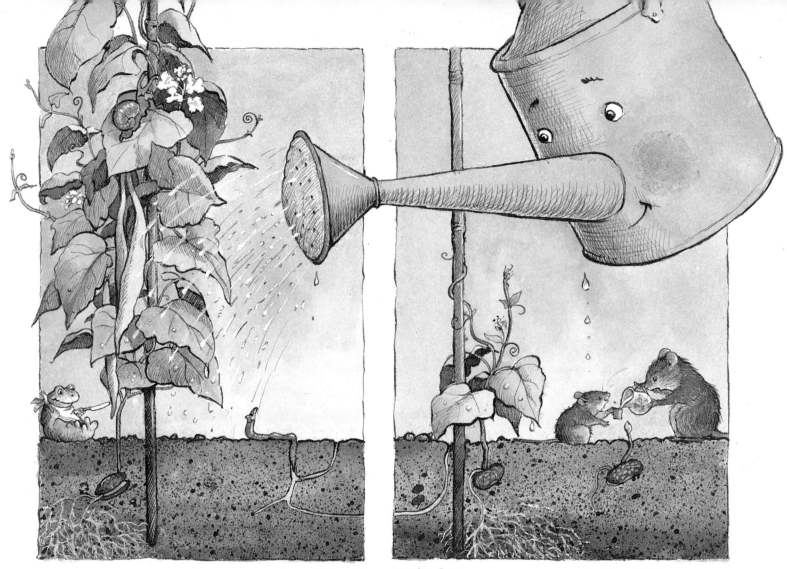

Willie loved his work. He had an important job. He helped plant the seeds and cuttings. In the hot summer he watered the garden when the flowers and vegetables were very thirsty.

He also loved talking with his friends in the tool shed.

  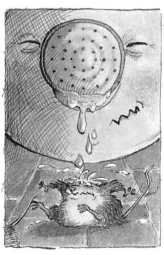 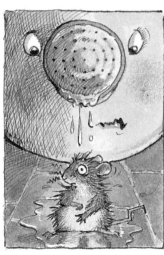

After Willie had been working in the garden, there was always water left inside the rose. One unhappy day his rose started to leak. Water dripped on to the floor of the shed and made a puddle.

When this happened every day it made the other tools
cross. They complained that Willie's puddle was making
the shed damp and them rusty.

Rumbles the roller was indeed rusty. He blamed Willie. The other tools agreed. Tears formed in Willie's eyes. He swallowed hard and blinked. "It's not my fault," he pleaded. "Don't shout at me. My rose is leaking."

Although the tools said they were sorry, they wiggled away from Willie's puddle. Poor Willie was left all alone. At night he would sit and quietly weep. His tears only made the puddle bigger.

The summer came. The days were long and hot. Willie was busy taking water to the flowers and vegetables.

Sometimes Henry, the gardener, left him in the greenhouse and the heat made him giddy.

The sun shone fiercely and for many weeks there was no rain. Willie was taken to the outside tap by Henry's cottage.

He had never been there before. He felt strange away
from his friends.

The other tools stayed in the shed because the earth was too dry and hard for them. The plants and flowers were desperately thirsty. They withered in the heat and some nearly died.

Willie was still busy.

Hour after hour, day after day, he watered the plants and flowers.

He was keeping the garden alive!

At last it rained. Willie was able to enjoy a well-earned rest in the shed. Even though water still dripped from his rose, the other tools turned and wiggled towards him. They knew he had saved the garden.

When Henry came into the shed later that day, he noticed the puddle. He saw that Willie's rose was leaking. He bought Willie a shiny new rose. All the tools shouted,
"Three cheers for Willie!"

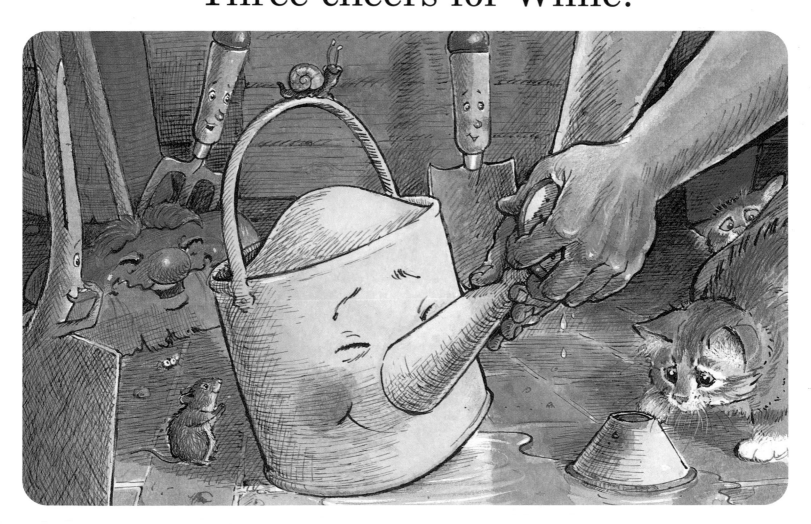

FURTHER

TALES FROM HENRY'S GARDEN

RUMBLES THE ROLLER
SPIRO THE SPADE
MUGGERIDGE THE MOWER